Star
of Wild Horse Canyon

by CLYDE ROBERT BULLA

illustrated by GRACE PAULL

cover by LYDIA ROSIER

SCHOLASTIC INC.
New York Toronto London Auckland Sydney Tokyo

To

Carlotta Lukins

of Ashtabula College

ISBN 0-590-09072-0

12 11 10 9 8 7 6 5 4 3 2 1   9   3 4 5 6 7/8

Contents

Wild Horses

A car was coming toward Starlight Ranch. Danny Hopper saw it on the side of the mountain as he rode his pony up from the pasture.

"Somebody's coming!" he called.

Danny's father came out of the ranch house. "Where?" he asked.

"Up there on our road," said Danny.

He was proud of the mountain road. Last year, when he and his father and mother came to Starlight Ranch, there had been rocks and bushes in the road. He and his father had dug out rocks and cut bushes. Now a car could come all the way to the ranch.

"That looks like your Uncle Mack's truck," said Father.

Danny kept his eyes on the car as it came down the mountain. "It *is* Uncle Mack!" he said. "Get up, Ginger. Let's go meet him."

He rode his pony down to the gate.

Uncle Mack drove up in his little green truck. On the side of the truck was BAR-K RANCH. That was the name of Uncle Mack's ranch on the other side of the mountain.

"Hello, Uncle Mack," said Danny.

Uncle Mack stopped the truck and said, "Hello." He looked at Danny's red shirt and his jeans and cowboy boots. "You're still a cowboy, I see."

"That's what I'm always going to be," said Danny.

"But you need another horse," said Uncle Mack.

"What for?" Danny looked at his spotted pony. "Ginger is a good little old pony."

"I know, but you're getting to be a big boy," said Uncle Mack, "and Ginger is just a little horse. Your legs are getting long. Pretty soon your feet are going to drag on the ground!"

"We can still beat you to the house — can't

we, Ginger? Come on!" Danny turned his pony around, and they were off. They went so fast that they *did* beat the truck to the ranch house.

"That wasn't fair," laughed Uncle Mack as he drove up. "I couldn't get my truck started soon enough."

Danny's mother came out on the porch. "You're just in time for supper," she said.

"I thought I would be," said Uncle Mack.

Danny rode Ginger to the pasture and turned him out for the night. When he went back to the house, supper was ready.

They ate in the kitchen. They had fried chicken and baked potatoes and carrots and peas. They had corn bread and honey and big glasses of cold milk. They had cherry pie.

When they had eaten, Uncle Mack pushed his chair back. He asked, "Have you ever been up in Juniper Canyon?"

"The canyon back of our ranch?" asked Father. "No, I haven't."

"Did you know there are wild horses there?" asked Uncle Mack.

Danny sat up straight. "Wild horses?"

"I knew there used to be some," said Father. "I thought they had all been caught long ago."

"There are some left," said Uncle Mack, "and I have a friend who wants some."

"What for?" asked Father.

"He wants them for a rodeo," said Uncle Mack.

"For the wild horse riding contests?" asked Danny.

"Yes," said Uncle Mack. "He wants about twenty horses. I told him I would get them for him. Some of the cowboys from my ranch are going to help. Will you help me, too?"

"Yes, I'll help," said Father.

"I'll help, too," said Danny.

"One of the biggest herds of wild horses runs in Juniper Canyon," said Uncle Mack. "It's not far away, but it's rough country and hard to get into."

"I have an idea," said Father. "If we go up to The Point, we can look down into the canyon. We can see how the land looks. Stay here all night, and we can start out early in the morning."

"I'll do that," said Uncle Mack. "But the road doesn't go all the way to The Point. We'll go in the truck as far as we can and walk the rest of the way."

Danny was so excited he could not keep still. "Are you going to take me?" he asked.

Father and Uncle Mack looked at each other.

"Shall we take him?" asked Uncle Mack.

"He might get tired," said Father.

"Then we would have to carry him on our

backs," said Uncle Mack, "and think what a big load he would be."

"I won't get tired," said Danny. Then he saw that Father and Uncle Mack were laughing. "You were going to take me all the time!" he said.

"Yes, we were," said Father. "Maybe Judy would like to go, too. Why don't you go and ask her?"

"All right, I will," said Danny.

At Judy's House

Danny ran out the back door and down
the hill to the little house where Judy Wicker
lived. He and Judy were in the same class at
school and they were good friends. Once Starlight Ranch had belonged to Judy's grandfather.
Last year he had sold it to Danny's father, but
he and Judy still lived there, in the little house
under the apple tree.

Danny knocked. Judy came to the door. She
wore a boy's shirt and jeans, but she had a red
ribbon in her long yellow hair.

"Hello, Danny," she said. "Come in."

Danny went in. At the table sat Judy's grandfather. He was cleaning his pistols. They were
old-fashioned pistols with pearl handles. He was
rubbing them with a soft cloth.

"How are you, Mr. Wicker?" asked Danny.

"Pretty well, thank you, young man," said Mr. Wicker.

Danny told Judy, "Uncle Mack is here. We're going up to The Point in the morning. Would you like to go with us?"

"Yes, I would," said Judy. "I know it's pretty up there, now that it's spring and all the trees are green again."

"Guess what we're going up there for," said Danny.

"I can't guess," she said.

"We're going to see about catching wild horses," said Danny.

"You *are!*" Judy was excited. "I knew there were wild horses in Juniper Canyon."

"That's where we're going to look," said Danny. "Judy, where do wild horses come from?"

Judy went to her grandfather. He was half-asleep in his chair. She put her hand on his arm. "Tell us about wild horses," she said.

"Wild horses?" Mr. Wicker pulled at his long white beard. "What do you want to know about them?"

"Where do they come from?" she asked.

"Were they always here, like deer and bears and rabbits?" asked Danny.

"No," said Mr. Wicker. "Before the white men came, the Indians had no horses. The white men brought the first ones to this country."

"On ships?" asked Danny.

"Yes, on ships," said Mrs. Wicker. "Some of them got away. They ran together in herds. They lived in the woods and canyons where no one could catch them. They lived away from men so long that they got to be wild horses. That was a long time ago, but there are still herds of wild horses in the West."

"I hope we see some tomorrow," said Danny.

"I hope so, too," said Mr. Wicker. "A herd of wild horses is a pretty sight. You won't soon forget it."

He closed his eyes, and his head nodded. He smiled.

"He's dreaming," said Danny.

"Yes," said Judy. "I think he's dreaming of the West — the way it was when he was a boy."

The Grew Ranch

Early in the morning they were ready to go. Father and Uncle Mack were in the front of the truck. Danny and Judy were in the back. They waved good-bye to Danny's mother and Judy's grandfather as the truck drove away.

For a while they drove through bright sunlight. Then the road ran through pine trees where the shade was deep and cool. Birds flew among the trees. Squirrels played in the branches.

"Look!" cried Danny.

"What is it?" asked Judy. "Oh, now I see!"

It was a deer running off through the trees.

"I like it up here," said Danny.

"So do I," said Judy. "When the wind blows through the pines, it makes the prettiest sound in the world."

They drove out of the woods, and the truck stopped.

Uncle Mack said, "This is as far as we can go in the car."

Danny and Judy jumped out. They were in front of a big old ranch house. There was no paint on the house. The barns and sheds looked ready to fall down, and some of the fences *had* fallen down. A few sheep were eating grass in the pasture.

"Where are we?" asked Danny.

"This is the Grew Ranch," said Uncle Mack.

A man came out of the house. He had a round, red face, and his hat was sitting on the back of his head.

"Hello, Mr. Grew," said Uncle Mack.

"Hello, yourself," said the man. A tall boy came out of the house behind him. Next came a little boy. Then three small girls came out and stood on the porch.

"Are they all your children?" asked Uncle Mack.

"Yes, all mine." Mr. Grew said to his boys and girls, "Speak to the people."

The tall boy said nothing. The little boy said, "Hello." The three girls ran back into the house.

"They always run and hide like that," said Mr. Grew. "They're scared to talk to anyone they don't know." He pointed to the tall boy. "This is my oldest one. His name is Ralph."

Still the boy said nothing. He was taller and older than Danny. His eyes were black, his face was thin. He looked as if he never smiled.

"And this is my baby." Mr. Grew pointed to the small boy. "He is just five years old. His name is Ben. He's not like his sisters. He's not scared of anything."

"Hello, Ben," said Danny.

"Hello," said Ben. "What's your name?"

"I'm Danny, and this is Judy," Danny told him.

"Danny and Judy — Danny and Judy!" sang Ben. He jumped around in a circle.

Ralph said in a low voice, "Don't be so silly!"

"I've got a horse," said Ben. "You want to see my horse?"

"Yes," said Danny.

"There he is, on the porch." Ben pointed to a big box with a saddle on it. "His name is Joe, and he's a good horse. He won't ever bite you or kick you."

"Don't talk so much," said Ralph.

Uncle Mack said to Mr. Grew, "We're going up to The Point. May we walk over your land?"

"Go right ahead," said Mr. Grew.

"I want to go, too," said Ben.

"I need you here," said Mr. Grew.

"All right. I'll stay with my horse." Ben climbed up on the box and sat in the saddle. He called good-bye to Danny and Judy as they started off across the pasture.

Juniper Canyon

Father and Uncle Mack led the way. On the other side of the pasture they found a trail that led up over the rocks. They began to climb.

Uncle Mack went first because he knew the way. Then came Father, Judy, and Danny. It was a long, hard climb. Three times they stopped to rest.

All at once Danny heard Uncle Mack call, "Here we are. This is The Point!"

In another moment they were all on top of a high rock. It was the biggest rock Danny had ever seen. It pointed out over Juniper Canyon like a big, flat arrowhead.

"Look how far we can see," said Judy.

"Miles and miles," said Danny. He looked down into the canyon.

The sides were steep and rocky. In the bottom of the canyon far below were juniper trees, and pines and cedars and oaks. Here and there were bare spots, like little pastures among the trees.

"Is this where the wild horses are?" asked Judy.

"Yes," said Uncle Mack.

"I don't see any," said Judy.

"I see *something*," said Danny. "Look — down in that bare spot!"

Father had brought his field glasses. He put them to his eyes.

"It's horses!" said Danny. "I can see them coming out from under the trees."

"He's right," said Father. "It *is* horses."

Uncle Mack looked through the field glasses. "That's a big herd. There must be thirty horses."

"May I see?" Judy looked through the glasses. "Oh, this makes them look big! Don't they look beautiful and wild! I'd like to be down there with them."

She handed the glasses to Danny. He put them to his eyes. "Now I can really see," he said. There were big horses and little horses. Some were black, some were gray, others were spotted. Most of them had black manes and tails. They looked thin, and they pulled up grass in big mouthfuls as if they were hungry.

"Do you see the black horse all by himself?" asked Father. "He's the scout. He looks and listens. If there is any danger, he whistles to tell the rest of the herd."

"Does he really whistle?" asked Judy.

"He blows the air out through his nose," said

Father. "It sounds like a whistle."

Danny was not looking at the scout. He was looking at another horse. It was the only white horse in the herd. It looked like a young horse. It had long legs and a proud head.

While Danny looked through the glasses, the scout pawed the ground. The herd turned and ran. In a moment not a horse was in sight.

"They're gone!" said Judy.

"Something made them run," said Uncle Mack. "Maybe it was a bear."

"Or maybe they saw us," said Father.

He and Uncle Mack began to talk about how they would catch the horses.

"See that little box canyon?" said Father. "There is only one way into it. We could run the horses in there and trap them."

"Let's ride up into the canyon tomorrow," said Uncle Mack, "and start to build our trap."

All the way down the trail, he and Father talked and made plans. Danny didn't hear them. All he could think about was the horse he had seen — the white horse with the proud head.

The Wild Horse
Roundup

When Danny and his father and Uncle Mack rode up into the canyon, Slim went with them. Slim was one of Uncle Mack's cowboys. He and Danny had been friends for a long time.

They were going to camp in the canyon. They had blankets and enough food to last three days. Each one had an ax, too. Sometimes they had to chop a trail through the trees and bushes.

Danny and Slim rode ahead.

"Do you think we are close to the wild horses?" asked Danny.

"I don't know," said Slim. "If they heard us coming, they're as far from us as they can get.

Nothing is wilder than a wild horse."

"I don't see how they live in the winter," said Danny. "We take good care of our horses. When it gets cold, we keep them in the barn and take feed to them. What do the wild horses do?"

"They know how to get along," said Slim. "They can paw through the snow and find grass. Sometimes they eat the bark off trees. Their hoofs get hard as iron from running over the rocks. They use their hoofs to break the ice and get water."

"Does anyone own these horses?" asked Danny.

"No. Wild horses belong to anyone who can catch them," said Slim.

About noon they came to a spring. The clear, cold water ran down over the rocks and into a pool. They stopped to drink and water their horses.

"This is a good place to make camp," said Uncle Mack.

They tied the horses under the trees. Danny brought a load of wood. Slim built a fire. Father fried some bacon and warmed up a can of beans. Uncle Mack made coffee.

While they ate, they talked about how to catch the wild horses.

"I think the best way is to build a fence across that box canyon we saw yesterday," said Father. "We need a fence with a gate in it. If we drive the horses in and shut the gate, we've got them."

"Make sure the fence is good and strong," said Slim. "When you run wild horses into a corral, they go over every inch of the fence. If they find one weak place, they break through."

After they had eaten, they washed their dishes in the pool and walked over to the box canyon.

"We can build a pole fence here where the box canyon is narrow," said Uncle Mack.

"Let's begin," said Slim.

They got their axes and cut poles from the trees.

For three days they cut poles. They made a big pile of them near the box canyon.

"That's enough for our fence," said Uncle

Mack. "Now we can go home."

Some of the other cowboys from Bar-K Ranch went up to build the fence.

It was a week before Danny and his father went back to the canyon. By that time the fence was built, with a gate in the middle. It was a strong fence. It was high enough that the horses could not jump over it.

Danny asked Uncle Mack, "Do you think we will catch all the herd of wild horses?"

"Yes, if we're lucky," said Uncle Mack.

"The white horse, too?" asked Danny.

"The white horse, too," said Uncle Mack.

"You told me once that Ginger wasn't big enough for me," said Danny. "You told me I needed another horse."

"Yes, I did say that," said Uncle Mack.

"I've been thinking about that white horse," said Danny. "I'd like to have him."

"You wouldn't want a wild horse," said Uncle Mack. "Wouldn't you rather have a good saddle horse, gentle and ready to ride?"

Before Danny could say any more, someone called Uncle Mack away, and the roundup had begun.

One day went by, and two more. Up and down, back and forth across Juniper Canyon the cowboys drove the wild horse herd. When a cowboy's horse grew tired, there was a fresh horse waiting. When one rider grew tired, there was another to take his place.

But the wild horses had no chance to rest. They grew more and more tired. They let the riders drive them closer to the box canyon.

On the morning of the fourth day, Danny was riding with the other cowboys. Father and Uncle Mack were riding, too.

Danny could see the whole herd now. He could see the white horse. The herd moved into the box canyon.

"We've got them!" shouted Uncle Mack. "Rush in!"

The riders rushed in. The wild horses ran down the box canyon, their manes and tails flying. The scout was in the lead. He came to the open gate and tried to stop, as if he knew there was danger. He squealed and stood on his hind legs. But all the other wild horses came from behind and carried him on inside the corral.

Slim jumped off his horse. He ran to the gate and pulled it shut.

And none too soon. The wild horses knew they had been trapped. They ran at the fence. They pawed at it and kicked it. But the fence was very strong. They could not break it down.

One horse tried to run up the side of the canyon. It was too steep to climb, and he fell back, kicking and squealing.

Danny's eyes were on the white horse. He stood with his back to the canyon wall. His neck and sides were wet with sweat. He looked frightened.

Danny was sorry for him. He thought, "If you were mine, I'd feed and water you and let you rest." He saw that the horse was all white except for a black star on his forehead. He thought, "If you were mine, I'd name you Star."

Father rode up to him. "The roundup is over for us, Danny. You've worked hard. Let's go home now and get some rest."

"I'd like to stay a little longer and look at Star," said Danny.

"Star?" said Father.

"The white horse."

"Oh. Uncle Mack said you liked him," said Father.

"Yes. Look at the way he holds his head. He's a proud horse."

"Yes, but he's wild, Danny," said Father. "He's not the right horse for a boy to have."

Uncle Mack rode up to them. "Why don't you two go home and get some rest?" he said. "I know you need it."

"We were just going," said Father.

"You did some good riding, Danny," said Uncle Mack. "You worked hard cutting poles for the fence, too. One of these days I'm going to bring you a present from Bar-K Ranch."

"Thank you, Uncle Mack," said Danny.

"How would you like a white-faced calf?" asked Uncle Mack.

"I'd like it fine," said Danny.

"Good. I'll see what I can find for you when I get back to the ranch," said Uncle Mack.

"Aren't you going back now?" asked Father.

"No," said Uncle Mack. "I'll camp here awhile and help the cowboys. Good-bye. I'll see you again in a few days."

Danny and his father said good-bye and rode away.

"How will they get the horses out of the canyon?" asked Danny.

"They'll rope them first and break them to lead," said Father. "Then they'll lead them out to the road and load them on trucks."

"Won't it take a long time?" asked Danny.

"Not so long," said Father. "Slim has a good trick. He ties a horse to a heavy piece of wood. The horse drags it around for a few days and gets used to the pull of a rope. After that he isn't so hard to lead."

Danny was quiet for a while.

"Are you still thinking about that white horse?" asked Father.

"Yes," said Danny. "I almost wish I'd never seen him, because now I can't keep from thinking about him."

"Try to forget about him," said Father.

"I'll try," said Danny, "but it's going to take a long time."

Uncle Mack's Present

It was Saturday, a week after the wild horse roundup. Danny was in town with his friend Jerry Bell. Jerry lived near Uncle Mack's ranch. He and Judy and Danny were all in the same class at school.

It was fun to go to town on Saturday. Danny liked to watch the people come in. They came on horseback. They came in cars and wagons. A few came on foot.

Danny and Jerry sat on a bench in front of the grocery store.

"Why do so many people come to town on Saturday?" asked Danny.

"I know why the cowboys come to town," said Jerry. "Most of them get paid on Saturday and they have money to spend."

"Maybe the other people come because they like to see each other," said Danny.

"Yes. They like to talk and hear all the news," said Jerry.

A big truck went down the street.

"It's a load of horses," said Jerry.

"That's one of Uncle Mack's cowboys driving the truck," said Danny. "Those are some of the wild horses! They're bringing them out of the canyon!"

They ran down the street after the truck. They hoped it would stop, but it went on. It went down the street and out of town.

"Uncle Mack must be sending them to the man he sold them to," said Danny. "Maybe Star was on that truck."

"Who?" asked Jerry.

"A white horse. I saw him up in the canyon and named him Star," said Danny. "I wonder if I'll ever see Star again."

Late in the afternoon Jerry and his father

brought Danny home. They let him out of the car in front of the gate. Danny walked up to the house.

Mother and Father were on the porch.

"Your Uncle Mack was just here," said Mother.

"Do you remember what he told you up in the canyon?" asked Father. "He said he wanted to give you a present."

"I remember," said Danny.

"He brought it today," said Father.

"I know what it is," said Danny. "He told me he was going to give me a calf. Is it a white-faced calf?"

"Come and see," said Father.

He and Mother went to the corral with Danny.

"Some day I'll have a big herd of white-faced cattle," said Danny. "I have three of my own now, and the calf will make —" He stopped. He looked. There was no calf in the corral. But there was something else. It was a white horse.

Danny said in a whisper, *Star!* Then he shouted, "It's Star — it's Star!"

The white horse jumped and ran to the other side of the corral. He shook his head and kicked at the gate.

"Is he — is he mine?" asked Danny.

"Yes," said Father. "Your Uncle Mack and I knew how much you wanted him, so we talked it over. At first we thought you were too young to have a horse like this. But your Uncle Mack said you rode like a man up in the canyon and you might as well have a man's horse."

Danny went up to the corral. "Star," he said. "You don't know me, do you?"

The horse backed away.

"But you *will* know me," said Danny.

He stood by the corral and looked at the horse. He stood there until Mother called him to supper.

After supper he went back. It was night, and the moon was high over the mountains. Danny climbed to the top of the corral fence and sat there.

"Star, you're not going to be a wild horse anymore," he said. "You won't have to dig through snow and ice to get grass and water. You'll be my horse and I'll take care of you."

The horse stood still in the bright moonlight. He held his head high as he sniffed the air and listened to the sound of Danny's voice.

A Wild Ride

In all the next few weeks Danny was never far from Star. He sat on the fence and talked to him. He fed him hay and oats. Once he held some grass through the corral gate. Star came up to the gate and backed away.

"Come on," said Danny. "You have to take it out of my hand."

And after a long time, Star did take the grass out of Danny's hand.

One day Danny went into the corral and threw a rope around Star's neck. At first Star pawed the dirt and kicked up his heels.

"Come on, boy," said Danny. "Nobody's going to hurt you."

He led Star across the corral. He tied him with his head close to a post. He patted him and put a halter on him.

Judy came up to the corral. "I don't see how you do that," she said. "He wouldn't let anyone else touch him."

"He's used to me. I'm around him so much he isn't afraid of me." Then Danny asked her, "Is there an old coat in the barn?"

"I think so," said Judy.

"Will you get it for me?" asked Danny.

Judy went into the barn and came out with an old coat. "What are you going to do with it?"

"I'll show you." Danny took the coat and laid it gently on Star's back.

"Now I see," said Judy. "You're getting him used to a saddle."

"Yes," said Danny. "See? He doesn't mind the coat at all."

The next day he put a blanket and saddle on Star. The horse turned his head and tried to see what was on his back. He shook himself.

"Easy!" said Danny, and the horse was quiet again. "Good boy," said Danny, and gave him some grass and hay.

Danny's father and Judy's grandfather came out to the corral.

"Look," said Judy. "Danny has a saddle on Star."

"See how gentle he is?" said Danny.

Judy's grandfather shook his head. "That horse has a wild look in his eye."

"He isn't wild now, Mr. Wicker," said Danny. "See how he lets me pet him? I think I could ride him. Will you let me ride him, Father?"

"Put a bridle on him," said Father. "I'll hold him while you get on. We'll see what he does."

Danny put the bridle over Star's head and slipped the bit into his mouth. Father held the reins.

"Be careful, Danny," said Judy.

"I will." Danny patted Star's neck. He pulled himself up slowly and got into the saddle.

The horse gave a little jump.

"It's all right, boy," said Danny.

The horse stood still.

"Will you lead him around, Father?" asked Danny.

Father led Star around the corral.

"He's not making any fuss at all," said Judy.

"No, he's not going to make any fuss," said Danny. "Let me ride him out into the pasture."

Father led Star out of the corral. He put the reins in Danny's hand.

"That horse has a wild eye," said Mr. Wicker. "I wouldn't trust him."

Star took a few short steps. He began to trot. Then he began to run.

"He's running away!" cried Judy.

"I knew he couldn't be trusted," said Mr. Wicker.

Down across the pasture went Star, with Danny bent low in the saddle.

"Did you see him jump that ditch?" said Judy. "Oh, what a wild ride! Can't we do something? He's going to run right on through the fence."

But at the far end of the pasture Star turned. He came racing back to the corral.

Father caught the bridle and stopped him.

"Are you all right, Danny?" he asked.

Danny nodded.

"We thought Star was running away with you," said Judy.

"No." Danny was out of breath. "He'd been shut up in the corral so long he wanted to run, so I let him. That was the best ride I ever had!"

A Stormy Night

Danny rode Star all over Starlight Ranch. He rode him to the well when he went to pump water for the cattle. He rode him when he drove the cattle to pasture. Sometimes he got up early and took a ride on Star before breakfast.

One day Danny's mother went into the kitchen and found Danny there. He had built a fire in the stove. He was cooking something in a big kettle.

"What are you doing?" she asked.

"I'm cooking dinner for my horse," he said.

"What!" said Mother.

"I'm making a sugar beet mash," said Danny.

"Uncle Mack told me how. He says it's good for horses."

"What is a sugar beet mash?" asked Mother.

"You cook some sugar beets and mash them up and mix them with oats," said Danny. "I want to see if Star likes it."

Star did like it. He liked it so much that Danny made him a sugar beet mash almost every day.

Father said to Danny, "I'm glad to see you take such good care of your horse. He doesn't look the way he did when he first came here."

"No," said Danny. "I brush him every day and comb his mane and tail. He gets more gentle all the time. He likes being a tame horse."

But Mr. Wicker was not so sure. "Young man, you watch that horse," he said. "He may act gentle but down inside he's still a wild horse. You can see it in his eyes and the way he holds his head."

"He really is tame, Mr. Wicker," said Danny.

But there were times when he was not so sure, either. Sometimes Star turned his head toward the canyon, as if he heard something

Danny could not hear. Sometimes late at night Star would neigh. Danny would sit up in bed and listen. It sounded like the wild horses neighing to each other in the canyon.

One summer morning Danny woke up and said to himself, "This is going to be a hot day."

He started to take a ride on Star but he went only a little way. It was too hot to ride. He turned Star out in the pasture.

All day it grew hotter.

"I wish it would rain," said Mother. "We need a rain to cool the air."

And that night there *was* rain. The wind blew. It howled in the trees and it howled down the chimney.

"I can feel the house shake," said Danny.

"If the wind blows much harder, it will blow the roof off," said Father.

"We'd better go to the storm cellar," said Mother.

Father lit the lantern and they went to the storm cellar back of the house. Judy and her grandfather went with them.

The storm cellar was a little room deep in the ground. It had stone steps and stone walls.

Mother had brought a blanket. She spread it on the floor and they sat down on it.

"The storm can't get us now," said Judy.

"We can't even hear it in the cellar," said Danny.

They sat around the lantern. They talked and sang and told stories until Father looked out and said, "The storm is over."

As they went up out of the cellar, Danny said, "I hope Star is all right."

"Don't worry about Star," said Father. "He knows how to take care of himself."

Danny was up early in the morning. There were sticks and leaves all over the yard. The wind had blown them there.

Danny ran to the pasture. Almost every morning Star was waiting at the gate. This morning he was not there.

"Star!" called Danny. "Where are you, Star?"

He climbed to the top of the gate. He could see all over the pasture, but the white horse was not in sight.

Across the pasture was a shed. Danny walked over to it and looked inside. It was empty.

Then he saw what had happened. Near the shed was an old cottonwood tree. The storm had torn off some branches and thrown them against the pasture fence. The fence was broken.

There were tracks where a horse had gone through the hole in the fence. Danny knew the tracks. They were Star's.

The Secret

Danny followed the tracks to the woods, and there among the rocks and pine needles he lost them.

"Star!" he called. "Here I am, Star!"

He listened for the sound of Star's steps, but all he heard was the echo of his own voice.

He went back to the house. He told Father, "The fence is broken, and Star is gone."

"Did you try to track him?" asked Father.

"Yes. He went into the woods," said Danny.

"Wait awhile, and don't worry," said Father. "I think Star will come home."

Danny tried not to worry. Almost every hour

he went out to look in the pasture. By the end of the day Star had not come home.

It was hard for Danny to sleep that night. He kept waking up and thinking about Star. "I wish I knew where he is," he thought. "I hope he comes home tonight."

But Star did not come home that night, or the next.

"He won't come back," said Mr. Wicker. "He's gone up into the canyons, back to the other wild horses."

"He isn't wild," said Danny. "He's tame now."

He went out to look for Star. He rode Ginger, his little spotted pony. Judy went with him. She rode her pony, Pepper. They went up and down the road and stopped at every ranch.

"Have you seen a white horse with a star on his forehead?" they asked, but no one had seen him.

They rode around the mountain to the Bell Ranch, and Jerry Bell helped them look. They looked all the rest of the day.

When Danny came home that evening, Father was sitting on the porch. "Did you have any luck?" he asked.

"No," said Danny.

"Your Uncle Mack and I have been looking, too," said Father. "We didn't have any luck, either."

"Do you think Star went back to the wild horses?" asked Danny.

"I don't know," said Father.

"Could we go up to Juniper Canyon and look?" asked Danny.

"No, Danny," said Father. "There are six or seven canyons where Star might be. It would take a year to look in them all. Even then we might not find him. But your uncle and I may round up more wild horses next spring. Maybe we can find you another horse."

"I don't want another horse," said Danny. "I want Star."

"Have you looked at the Grew Ranch yet?" asked Father.

"I don't think Star is there," said Danny. "There is a fence between here and the Grew Ranch. I don't think Star would have jumped over the fence."

"Maybe the Grews have seen him or know something about him," said Father. "Why don't you go over there tomorrow and ask?"

"All right," said Danny. "I will."

The next day he and Judy went to the Grew Ranch. They tied their ponies outside the gate and started up to the house.

A dog barked, and Mr. Grew came out of the barn. The tall boy, Ralph, came out behind him.

"Well, well!" said Mr. Grew. "Glad to see you again. What are you doing up here so far from home?"

"We're looking for a horse," said Danny.

"Did you lose a horse?" asked Mr. Grew.

"Yes. A white horse with a black star on his

forehead," said Danny. "Have you seen him?"

Mr. Grew shook his head. "No, I haven't. Ralph, have you — ?" He looked around. Ralph was gone. "Where did that boy go?"

"He went around the barn," said Judy.

"Well, I guess he didn't see any white horse or he'd have said so," said Mr. Grew. "I'm sorry you lost him. If I see him, I'll let you know."

"Thank you, Mr. Grew," said Danny.

He and Judy went back to where they had left their ponies.

They heard a shout, "Danny and Judy! Danny and Judy!"

Little Ben Grew had come out of the house and was running toward them.

"Did you come to play with me?" he asked.

"No, Ben. I came to look for my horse," said Danny.

"Did you lose your horse?" asked Ben.

"Yes," said Danny. "He ran away."

"See my horse, there on the porch?" Ben pointed to the box with the saddle on it. "He never runs away. His name is Joe. What's your horse's name?"

"Star," said Danny. "He's white with a black star on his forehead. If you see him, will you let me know?"

"Yes, I will," said Ben. "Where did you get your horse? Did you buy him at a store?"

"No," said Danny. "He was a wild horse. Do you remember the other time we came here? We went up on The Point and looked into the canyon at the wild horses. That's where I first saw my horse."

"I want to go see the wild horses," said Ben. "Will you take me?"

"It's too far," said Danny. "We have to go home now."

"Let's give him a ride first," said Judy. She asked Ben, "Do you want to ride my pony?"

"Yes," said Ben.

"Put your foot in my hand," said Judy. "There! Up you go!"

She helped him into the saddle and got on behind him. "We'll ride down to that little oak tree and back."

Danny rode beside Judy and Ben.

"I like your horse," said Ben. "I like him better than Ralph's."

"Does your brother have a horse like yours?" asked Judy.

"Oh, no. He has a real horse," said Ben. "But don't tell him I told you. It's a secret."

"Why is it a secret?" asked Danny.

"I don't know," said Ben. "Maybe he doesn't want anyone else to ride it. He hides it down here in the woods."

Danny sat up straight in the saddle. "How long has he had this horse?" he asked.

"Not very long," said Ben.

Danny and Judy looked at each other.

"Ben, we want to see this horse," said Danny. "Will you take us to see it?"

"Yes," said Ben, "but don't tell Ralph."

They tied their ponies to the little oak tree. Ben climbed the fence. Danny and Judy climbed the fence after him. They walked through the woods.

"Ralph ties his horse to a tree," said Ben. "He ties it with a long rope so it can get lots of grass. He rides it every day. I saw him riding it one day, and he told me it was a secret."

Judy whispered to Danny, "Do you think it's Star?"

"It must be," whispered Danny.

Ben stopped. "I hear Ralph coming. He's riding his horse. Hide!"

They hid in the bushes. Danny and Judy peeped out. Danny heard the horse's steps coming nearer. They sounded like Star's. He held his breath.

Ralph came into sight, riding his horse. It was not a white horse. It was brown, with a brown mane and tail.

Ralph rode quickly by. As soon as he was gone, Danny, Judy, and Ben came out of the bushes.

"Did you see the horse?" asked Ben.

"Yes," said Danny.

"It isn't very pretty, is it?" said Ben.

"No," said Danny.

"But Ralph says it's a good horse," said Ben.

Danny and Judy took Ben back to the house. They told him good-bye.

"Good-bye," said Ben. "Don't tell the secret."

"We won't," said Judy.

She and Danny rode away. They were tired and disappointed.

"Where shall we look tomorrow?" asked Judy.

"There's no place left to look," said Danny.

"Are you going to give up?" asked Judy.

"What else can I do?" said Danny. "I can't find my horse. He doesn't come back to me. What else can I do?"

Ben

The next morning Danny said nothing about Star. Mother and Father said nothing about him, either.

After breakfast Father said, "I have to go to town. We need feed for the chickens and salt for the cattle. Do you want to go along with me, Danny?"

"No, I'll stay and hoe in the garden before the sun gets hot," said Danny.

Father drove off to town alone. Danny went to the garden back of the house. He hoed all the weeds out of the tomatoes. He had started on the beans when he heard someone call, "Danny! Danny!"

It was Judy. She came running up to the garden fence. Behind her was Jerry Bell.

"Jerry came to tell us about little Ben Grew," said Judy.

"He's lost," said Jerry. "He's been gone all night. A man came to our house to tell us. My father said to tell you. They need people to help look for Ben."

"I'm going to help look," said Judy. "Grandfather said I could."

"I'll help, too," said Danny. "I know Mother will let me."

In a little while they were on their ponies, riding toward the Grew Ranch. "How did Ben get lost?" asked Danny.

"He was in the woods with his brother Ralph," said Jerry. "All at once Ben was gone. Ralph thought he had gone back to the house, but he hadn't. No one knows where he went."

"How long has he been gone?" asked Danny.

"Since yesterday," said Jerry. "Ralph thinks he is to blame because he let Ben get lost. He took a lantern and went out and looked all night."

Judy said, as they rode up to the Grew Ranch, "There must be a lot of people here. Look at all the cars and horses."

They went to the house. A woman came to the door. She looked as if she had been crying. The three small girls peeped out from behind her. They looked as if they had been crying, too.

"Are you Ben's mother?" asked Danny.

"Yes," said the woman.

"We came to help look for Ben," said Danny. "Have they found him yet?"

"No," said the woman. "They are looking for him in the woods."

Danny stopped. "I don't think Ben is in the woods," he said.

"Have they looked up toward The Point?" asked Danny.

"No," said the woman. "He's never played there."

"We'll go to the woods and help look," said Jerry.

"Oh, thank you," said the woman. "I hope you find him soon. Poor little Ben! He must be so hungry and afraid."

"Poor little Ben," said Judy, as they started to the woods.

"Where do you think he is?" asked Judy.

"Do you remember what he said to us yesterday?" said Danny. "He wanted to know all about Star and where he came from. I think he ran away from Ralph and started up to The Point to see the wild horses."

"You may be right," said Judy.

"Let's go to The Point," said Jerry.

They walked across the pasture and found the trail to The Point. They climbed up over the rocks and through the bushes.

The sun was hot on their heads. The trail grew harder to climb. It was a long time before they came out on The Point.

They stood on the big, flat rock. They looked out over Juniper Canyon.

"Here we are," said Judy.

"But where is Ben?" asked Jerry.

"Ben!" called Danny. "Where are you, Ben?"

"It won't do any good to call him," said Jerry. "He's not here, or we could see him."

"*Listen!*" said Judy.

They stood very still. A voice came to them. "I'm down here."

"It's Ben," said Judy.

"Where is he?" Jerry looked all around.

Danny lay flat on the big rock and looked
over the edge.

On the side of The Point was a shelf of rock.
There on the shelf sat Ben.

"Danny!" said Ben. "Take me home."

"Hold up your hand," Danny told him.

Ben held up his hand, but Danny could not
quite reach it.

"I wish we had a rope," said Jerry.

"Can you and Judy let me down over the rock a little farther?" asked Danny.

"Yes, we can do that," said Judy.

She held one of Danny's legs. Jerry held the other. They kept him from falling while he reached over the edge of the rock.

"Reach up to me, Ben," said Danny.

Ben held up his arms. Danny caught hold of them. He said to Judy and Jerry, "Pull!"

They pulled as hard as they could. They pulled Ben off the shelf and up on top of The Point.

"Danny and Judy!" he said. He looked at Jerry. "Who are you?"

"I'm Jerry. Are you all right, Ben?"

"Yes." Ben pointed down to the shelf. "But I'm not going down *there* anymore."

"How did you get down there?" asked Danny.

"I came to see the wild horses, but I never saw any," said Ben. "I was looking, and I fell down there, and I couldn't get up again. I don't want to stay all night down there anymore." Tears came into his eyes. "I'm hungry," he said.

"We'll take you home," said Judy. "Here —
get on my back."

They took turns carrying him down the trail.
When they came to the pasture, he said, "I can
walk."

His mother saw them coming. She came running across the pasture.

"Ben! My little boy!" she cried, and picked
him up in her arms.

"We found him up on The Point," said
Danny.

"Thank you for finding him," said Ben's
mother. "Thank you a thousand times!"

She carried him to the house and put him down on the porch. Then she rang the big dinner bell in front of the house to let everyone know that Ben was safe at home again.

A Visit from Ralph

It was the day after Ben had been found. Danny was working in the garden. He was hoeing the weeds out of the beans.

His mother called him. "Will you come here, Danny?"

He went to the house.

"Look down by the gate," she said. "There's someone on a horse."

Danny was surprised. "It looks like Ralph Grew."

"He just stands there," said Mother. "Why doesn't he come in?"

"He acts as if he's afraid," said Danny.

"Why should he be afraid?" asked Mother.

"I don't know. I'll go talk to him." Danny went down to the gate.

Ralph was on the horse Danny had seen him riding in the woods. There was no saddle on the horse — only an old bridle made of rope.

"Hello," said Danny.

"Hello." Ralph got off the horse. He stood there with his hand on the bridle. "I want to thank you," he said, "because you found my little brother."

"I was glad I could help find him," said Danny.

Ralph led the horse forward. "Here," he said. "He's yours."

He tried to put the bridle reins in Danny's hand. Danny would not take them.

"Oh, no, Ralph," he said. "You can't give me your horse just because I helped find your brother."

"It isn't my horse," said Ralph. "It's yours."

Danny looked at the horse. "He looks like Star!" he said.

The horse pawed the dirt and lifted his head. He looked more like Star than ever.

"But the horse I lost is white," said Danny. "This horse is brown."

"He wasn't brown when I found him," said Ralph. "It was the day after the big storm. I found him in the woods by our ranch. There was a bad cut on his leg. You can see the mark."

"Yes, I see it," said Danny.

"I guess he jumped the fence and cut his leg," said Ralph. "I took care of him. I got to like him. I always wanted a horse of my own and I never had one, and I — I wanted this one for mine. I hid him in the woods. But I was afraid someone would see him and say, 'That's the white horse I lost,' and take him away from me. So I colored him brown."

"You *what?*" said Danny.

"I colored him brown," said Ralph. "I boiled the bark of some trees and made dye — like the Indians do. I made a lot of dye and put it all over him."

"Now I can see," said Danny. "There is the star on his forehead. I can see it through the dye."

"I didn't know he was yours till the day you came looking for him," said Ralph. "I tried to tell you, but I liked him so much I...I wanted to keep him a little longer. Then you came and

found my little brother, and I was so ashamed I couldn't stand it. I just had to bring your horse back."

"Star!" Danny put his arms around the horse's neck. "Now I know you."

"The dye will grow out," said Ralph. "It won't be long till he's a white horse again. I'm sorry I kept him so long and made you worry."

"I did worry," said Danny, "but I'm glad you found him and took care of him when he was hurt."

Ralph said good-bye to Star. He said good-bye to Danny. He started down the road.

"Wait," said Danny.

Ralph turned around.

"I think Uncle Mack is going to round up more wild horses next spring," said Danny. "I'll ask him to keep one for you."

Ralph's eyes opened wide. "You *will?*"

"Yes. The next time I see him, I'll talk to him about it." Danny jumped on Star's back. He rode up toward the house. "Look, everyone — look!" he shouted.

Father came out of the barn. Mother came

out of the ranch house. Judy and Mr. Wicker came out of the little house under the apple tree.

"It's Star!" said Danny. "He's come home."

And Star shook his mane and held his head high.